Overcoming the Odds

Hakeem Olajuwon

Suzanne J. Murdico

RSVP ®

RAINTREE STECK-VAUGHN
P U B L I S H E R S
The Steck-Vaughn Company

Austin, Texas

Published by Raintree Steck-Vaughn Publishers,
an imprint of Steck-Vaughn Company

Developed for Steck-Vaughn Company by
Visual Education Corporation, Princeton, New Jersey
Editor: Marilyn Miller
Photo Research: Marty Levick
Electronic Preparation: Cynthia C. Feldner
Production Supervisor: Ellen Foos
Electronic Production: Lisa Evans-Skopas, *Manager;*
Elise Dodeles, Deirdre Sheean, Isabelle Verret
Interior Design: Maxson Crandall

Raintree Steck-Vaughn Publishers staff
Editor: Kathy DeVico
Project Manager: Joyce Spicer

Photo Credits: **Cover:** © Ira Strickstein/Reuters/Bettmann;
4: © Ira Strickstein/Reuters/Bettmann; 7: © Tim DeFrisco/NBA Photos; 10: © UPI/Bettmann;
12: © Bill Baptist/NBA Photos; 18: © UPI Bettmann; 19: © Brian Christopher/UPI/Bettmann;
22: © Walt Frerck/UPI/Bettmann; 23: © Calvin Horn/UPI/Bettmann;
25: © Debra Myrent/UPI/Bettmann; 28: © Andrew D. Bernstein/NBA Photos;
29: © Bill Baptist/NBA Photos; 31: Bruno Torres/UPI/Bettmann;
33: Courtesy of the Dream Foundation; 34: © Mazlan Enjah/Reuters/Bettmann;
36: Courtesy of the Dream Foundation; 38: Ray Stubblebine/Reuters/Bettmann;
41: © Michael Boddy/Reuters/Bettmann; 43: © Gamma

Library of Congress Cataloging-in-Publication Data
Murdico, Suzanne J.
    Hakeem Olajuwon / Suzanne J. Murdico.
        p.   cm. — (Overcoming the odds)
    Includes bibliographical references (p. 46) and index.
    Summary: Relates how Hakeem Olajuwon overcame many obstacles to become one
of the best centers in the NBA.
    ISBN 0-8172-4131-0 (hardcover)
    ISBN 0-8172-8002-2 (softcover)
    1. Olajuwon, Hakeem, 1963–   —Juvenile literature. 2. Basketball players—United
States—Biography—Juvenile literature. 3. Houston Rockets (Basketball)—Juvenile
literature. [1. Olajuwon, Hakeem, 1963–   . 2. Basketball players. 3. Nigerian
Americans—Biography.]   I. Title. II. Series.
GV884.O43M87 1998
796.323′092—dc21
[B]   97–27930
                                                                                        CIP
                                                                                        AC

Printed and bound in the United States
1 2 3 4 5 6 7 8 9 0   WZ   01 00 99 98 97

Table of Contents

Chapter 1

Living the Dream

The Houston Rockets were struggling. They had won the 1994 National Basketball Association (NBA) championship. Now they wanted to win a second title. Early in the 1994–1995 season, though, things started going badly.

By midseason, several top Houston players were replaced. The Rockets traded forward Otis Thorpe to the Portland Trail Blazers. In exchange, the Rockets received guard Clyde Drexler and forward Tracy Murray. Carl Herrera, a Houston forward, was injured and missed most of the season's second half. In addition, guard Vernon Maxwell took a sudden leave of absence. He was unhappy because he felt he was being overshadowed by Drexler, the new guard.

So many lineup changes in the middle of the season can be hard on a team. The players often have trouble adjusting. It can be difficult for them to come together as a team.

Even worse, the Rockets' star center—Hakeem "The Dream" Olajuwon—was playing below par. At

In game four of the 1995 National Basketball Association finals, Hakeem towers over Orlando Magic center Shaquille O'Neal (right) and guard Dennis Scott (left).

6 feet 11 inches tall and 255 pounds, Hakeem was not the biggest of the "big men" in the NBA. But he ranked as one of the greatest basketball players in history.

Unlike many centers, Hakeem is quick, nimble, and graceful. One magazine reporter wrote, "No center in the NBA has the spins and twirls and fakes that Olajuwon has."

Every year Hakeem perfected a new aspect of his game. He now had so many moves that he kept his opponents guessing. "I see my game as something creative, maybe something new," he said. "More moves, more fakes, more of the unexpected."

Hakeem had been playing with the Rockets for 11 seasons. He had led the team to its first NBA championship in 1994. That year he was also named the league's Most Valuable Player (MVP) for the regular season and for the finals.

Now, though, something was wrong with him. Suddenly he looked tired. He seemed to have lost his usual enthusiasm for running up and down the court, jumping, and sinking baskets. At age 32, Hakeem was no longer young for a basketball player. Although many players continue to play in their 30s, maybe Hakeem's best years were over.

But Hakeem himself found the cause of the problem. A devout Muslim, he had fasted during the Muslim holy month of Ramadan. He was not eating between daybreak and sundown. This lack of food had caused Hakeem to develop a medical condition

Hakeem sits on the bench with teammate Clyde Drexler.

called anemia. A person who is anemic feels tired all the time.

Doctors gave Hakeem pills to treat his anemia and told him to rest for two weeks. Soon Hakeem was back to his old self. But would it be in time for the Rockets? It looked as if the team might not even make it into the playoffs.

When the 1994–1995 regular season ended, Houston's record of wins and losses was 47–35. This put the team in sixth place in the Western Conference. During the 1993–1994 season, the Rockets had won 58 games and placed first in the conference. Nevertheless, with Hakeem healthy again, the team managed to make it into the 1995 conference playoffs.

In the playoffs 16 teams qualify to compete for the NBA championship. Eight teams are from the Eastern Conference and 8 are from the Western

Conference. The first round is the best of a five-game series, whereas the other rounds are the best of a seven-game series. The winners of the first round advance to the conference semifinals and then, if they win, to the conference finals. The winner of the Eastern Conference meets the winner of the Western Conference in the NBA finals.

In the first round of the 1995 playoffs, the Rockets faced the Utah Jazz. Even though the Jazz were seeded, or ranked, third in the conference, the Rockets defeated them. Hakeem led the way, scoring 40 points and 33 points in the final two games.

In the conference semifinals, the Rockets met the second-seeded Phoenix Suns, led by the talented Charles Barkley. The Suns were very tough opponents. The Rockets were behind three games to one. Then, in a thrilling comeback, Houston won three games in a row and advanced to the conference finals.

Now the Rockets faced an even greater challenge: the top-seeded San Antonio Spurs. The Spurs' regular-season record of 62–20 was the best in the NBA. And their star player, David Robinson, had won that season's MVP award. But Hakeem outplayed Robinson during their matchup. While Robinson averaged only 25.5 points a game, Hakeem averaged 35.3 points. The Rockets beat the Spurs in six games.

Rockets' coach Rudy Tomjanovich was proud of his star center. He said that Hakeem had given "a legendary performance."

The Rockets' opponents in the NBA finals were the Orlando Magic. After seeing Hakeem's performance against the Spurs, the Magic coaching staff realized that they were dealing with a powerful force. "Hakeem was incredible, absolutely incredible," said Magic coach Brian Hill. "He has put that team on his shoulders and carried it through the playoffs."

Even Shaquille O'Neal, the Magic's 7-foot 1-inch center, was awed. "Hakeem is the best center in the league," he said.

Hakeem and O'Neal were evenly matched, but the Rockets prevailed. In four straight games, they beat the Orlando Magic to win their second straight NBA championship. For the second year in a row, Hakeem was named NBA finals MVP.

When people talk about his skills on the basketball court, Hakeem is often compared to such great stars of the past as Kareem Abdul-Jabbar and Wilt Chamberlain. But in many ways, Hakeem is very different from most other players in the NBA.

Many young basketball hopefuls start dribbling the ball soon after they learn to walk. Hakeem did not pick up a basketball until he was 16 years old. A year later he came to the United States from his home in a poor African country. He moved thousands of miles away from his family. Before he could become the basketball star he is today, Hakeem had to overcome many obstacles.

Chapter 2

Journey from Africa

Hakeem Abdul Olajuwon is from Nigeria. With 98 million people, Nigeria has a larger population than any other country in Africa. Hakeem was born on January 21, 1963, in Lagos, Nigeria's largest city. He is the third child of Salam and Abike Olajuwon. Hakeem has four brothers and one sister.

The Olajuwon family lived in a red brick house with three bedrooms. Hakeem's parents owned a cement business. They operated the business from

This is the Marini, the main street of Lagos, Nigeria.

their home. "They taught us to be honest, work hard, respect our elders, believe in ourselves," said Hakeem. The Olajuwons brought up their children as Muslims.

Hakeem and his brothers and sister attended a school near their home. While Hakeem was growing up, he learned to speak English, French, and four Nigerian dialects. The word *Olajuwon* means "always on top" in Arabic. *Hakeem* means "doctor" or "wise one."

As a child Hakeem was quiet and shy. He enjoyed playing sports. Because basketball is not nearly as popular in Nigeria as it is in the United States, Hakeem played team handball and volleyball. He was also a talented soccer goalie and cricket player. Cricket is a team sport played with a ball, bats, and wickets, or wooden posts.

Hakeem did not pick up a basketball until 1979. One day a basketball coach asked him if he would be interested in playing basketball. Hakeem did not know much about basketball. He had not even seen it played on television. However, he had read and heard stories about legendary players like Kareem Abdul-Jabbar and Magic Johnson of the Los Angeles Lakers. Hakeem thought that he might enjoy the sport.

Hakeem began practicing with the Nigerian national basketball team. "I did not know any of the rules," he said. "I just knew that this game seemed to

As a youngster, Hakeem played cricket in Nigeria.

combine all the things I liked from the other games: the footwork, the running, and the jumping."

Although Hakeem did not start playing basketball until he was 16, he did have one huge advantage. By that age, Hakeem was nearly seven feet tall. Of course, although height is very important, by itself it does not make anyone a great basketball player. That takes talent, skill, and a lot of practice.

Hakeem practiced and learned quickly. The hard work paid off. Only one year later, he played on Nigeria's national basketball team in the 1980 Junior All-Africa Games.

Hakeem was soon spotted by Chris Pond, an American who coached a Central African basketball team. Pond could see that Hakeem's game was a bit rough around the edges. But he immediately recognized that the teenager had raw talent. The coach offered to help Hakeem obtain a basketball scholarship to an American college. If Hakeem played basketball on a college team, he could attend school for free.

This sounded like a good idea to Hakeem. His parents had taught him about the value of education. And he knew that the United States had many excellent colleges. He also knew, though, that he probably would not be able to attend one of these colleges without a scholarship.

At first Hakeem's parents were not sure about the idea of their son playing basketball. They had never even seen a basketball game. "I did not want to encourage my son in basketball because I did not know the value," said Hakeem's father. Soon, however, Hakeem's parents realized that playing basketball was a way for their son to receive a college education in the United States.

So Hakeem prepared for his journey to America. "I was looking forward to it, and I was excited," he recalled. "It's been the goal of my generation in Nigeria that they study abroad, so I was not scared."

Still, it was a big step for the young Nigerian to leave all he knew behind him. What would lie ahead for him in a strange country?

Chapter 3

A Difficult Adjustment

Hakeem flew to the United States to look at several possible schools. His first stop was New York City. When Hakeem arrived, he realized that there was a new obstacle in his path: the weather. It was a very cold and windy day in October 1980. The weather in Nigeria is warm all year-round, so Hakeem was not used to the climate in New York. He was wearing only lightweight clothing, and he was freezing.

Right then and there, Hakeem decided that he did not want to go to school in New York..He turned around and boarded another plane to his next stop— Houston, Texas. In Houston the weather was much warmer. Hakeem thought that he would like to live there. He went to visit the University of Houston.

The coach of the basketball team, the Houston Cougars, was Guy Lewis. Coach Lewis knew that basketball was not played exactly the same way in other countries as it was in the United States. Hakeem would have to adjust his game. But would he be able to do so? At first Lewis wasn't sure if Hakeem would be able to compete against American players.

But once Coach Lewis saw Hakeem play basketball, he changed his mind. He recognized that Hakeem had awesome potential. The coach offered Hakeem a scholarship to the University of Houston, and Hakeem accepted. He would study business technology and play basketball for the Cougars.

In January 1981, Hakeem started taking classes at the university. During that first season, Hakeem was "redshirted." That meant that he had to sit on the bench and not play with the team.

Coach Lewis felt that Hakeem needed more practice playing American-style basketball. "I don't care how you slice it," said the coach. "He flat-out didn't know how to play." So besides adjusting to school in a new country, Hakeem had to start nearly from scratch when it came to basketball.

In addition, Hakeem needed to build up his body and his endurance. At nearly seven feet tall and only 190 pounds, Hakeem was very thin. After playing basketball for only five or ten minutes, Hakeem would become tired and sore.

Part of the problem was that Hakeem did not stretch first before playing. It is most important for athletes to loosen up before a game. After Hakeem started stretching to warm up, he was able to play without becoming sore. He also started working out with weights to improve his strength.

Another problem was American food. Hakeem missed Nigerian foods, such as *fufu,* which is baked dough topped with stew. He also longed for the large fried bananas called *dodos*.

But Hakeem soon found new foods to enjoy. He liked fried chicken, oysters, and especially ice cream. He even carried an ice chest filled with ice cream around the college campus.

Hakeem's improved appetite combined with his weight lifting paid off. Over time he filled out to 255 pounds and increased his muscle tone.

The food in the United States was not the only obstacle that Hakeem had to overcome. Some social customs in Nigeria are very different from customs in this country. Hakeem's teammates teased him about certain customs, such as bowing to people who were older than he was. His teammates thought such habits were unusual or old-fashioned.

"I was brought up to honor and respect older people," explained Hakeem. "I bow to them out of respect. They laughed at me, so I stopped."

Adapting to a new life in a new country would be difficult for almost anyone. For Hakeem, however, it was especially trying. He was thousands of miles away from his family and friends. On top of that, he was painfully shy.

"He got unnerved when people weren't patient with him," recalled Clyde Drexler, one of Hakeem's teammates. "I think he was homesick a lot. But we helped him, taught him our ways. He watched everything we did. He was a hawk."

Not all of Hakeem's adjustments were difficult, though. Some things were better in the United States. In Nigeria, Hakeem had always had trouble finding sneakers that were big enough. The largest size he could find was a 14, and that was too small. He had to break in the sneakers for a month before he could play basketball in them. In the United States, size 16 sneakers were easy to buy. When Hakeem tried them on, he was amazed.

"It was the first time I wore shoes that felt like that," he said. "They felt like I had no shoes on at all!"

Hakeem was determined to overcome all the obstacles that stood in his way. During the summer he spent a lot of time practicing at the Fonde Recreation Center in downtown Houston.

When the basketball season began in the fall of 1981, Hakeem was finally a member of the Cougars. Yet Coach Lewis did not feel that he was ready to be in the starting lineup. But throughout the year, Hakeem's skills steadily improved. Toward the end of the season, the coach put him in six games as starting center. Fans and reporters were immediately impressed by the young Nigerian.

The Cougars played well enough to earn a spot in the National Collegiate Athletic Association (NCAA) tournament. There they started a winning streak that carried them all the way to the Final Four. The Final Four is the semifinal round. The winners of the two semifinal matches compete for the NCAA title.

Eighteen-year-old Hakeem practiced hard at the University of Houston.

HOME OF THE
COUGARS

The Cougars did not make it past the semifinals, however. They lost to the University of North Carolina, a team that included Michael Jordan.

Once again Hakeem spent much of his summer in Houston, playing basketball at the Fonde Recreation Center. When he returned for the 1982–1983 season, he saw a lot more action. From the way Hakeem was playing, Coach Lewis knew that he was ready to be the Cougars' starting center.

Other people were beginning to notice this talented player. They began calling him "Hakeem the Dream." And the Cougars earned the nickname "Phi Slama Jama" because one of their favorite moves was the slam dunk. (Phi Slama Jama was a takeoff on names of college fraternities, such as Phi Gamma Delta.)

During the regular season, the Cougars' record was 27–2. They were ranked number one in the country and qualified for another try at the NCAA championship. With Hakeem leading the way, the Cougars made it into the Final Four. Then they defeated Louisville to advance to the finals.

In the championship game, Houston faced North Carolina State. Although North Carolina took the lead in the first half, Houston rallied in the second half. With only two minutes remaining, the score was tied at 52–52. Just as the buzzer sounded, however, North Carolina slam-dunked a shot to win.

The loss was a terrible disappointment for Hakeem and the Cougars. "I try not to think about the last minute," Hakeem said later. "I feel too bad just mentioning it. It was heartbreaking."

Hakeem had played remarkably well during the tournament. In that final game, he had an impressive 20 points, 18 rebounds, and 11 blocks. Hakeem was named the Most Valuable Player in the NCAA tournament. He was the first player from a losing team to earn that honor in 17 years.

Once again Hakeem returned to Fonde during the off-season. That summer many of the players noticed that Hakeem had developed a lot more confidence in his game.

Hakeem brought his newfound confidence and ever-improving skills back to the Cougars. During the 1983–1984 season, the Cougars' record was 28–4. Hakeem and his teammates had another opportunity to win an NCAA championship.

Once again Hakeem led the Cougars into the finals. There they were matched against Patrick Ewing and the Georgetown Hoyas. In the end Georgetown won the championship with a score of 84–75. And once again Hakeem and the Cougars returned to Houston without an NCAA title.

After this third season with the Cougars, Hakeem made a big decision. He chose to leave the university, without graduating and earning a degree, to start a career as a professional basketball player for the Houston Rockets. Even though he had started playing so late and had had to learn the American style of basketball from scratch, Hakeem felt that he was ready to join the NBA.

Chapter 4

Shooting Like a Rocket

During the 1983–1984 season, the Houston Rockets had the worst record in the Western Conference of the NBA. At that time the team with the worst record in each conference took part in a coin toss. The winner gained first choice in the college draft. The Houston Rockets won the coin toss in 1984.

That year the players in the college draft included some incredible athletes: Hakeem Olajuwon, Michael Jordan, and Charles Barkley. With first pick, Houston selected Hakeem. Michael Jordan was third pick, chosen by the Chicago Bulls. And Charles Barkley was the fifth draft choice, picked by the Philadelphia 76ers.

Hakeem was happy to be chosen by the Rockets. He liked Houston and could now continue to live there. The Rockets signed Hakeem to a contract in which he would earn $7 million over six years.

With this newfound wealth, Hakeem decided to make some investments. He invested in gas, oil, and real estate. He also spent some of the money on luxuries, such as several Mercedes-Benz cars.

Here Hakeem stands next to his new Mercedes just after hearing by phone that he would be playing NBA basketball for the Houston Rockets.

When the Rockets drafted Hakeem in 1984, the team already had a center. He was Ralph Sampson, who was 7 feet 4 inches tall.

Although Olajuwon is shorter than Sampson, Houston decided to make him the center because of his greater power. They moved Sampson to the forward position. These two players soon became known as the "Twin Towers" because they were so tall.

Once more Hakeem had to make a quick adjustment, this time to life in the NBA. Hakeem was shy and gentle, but his teammates helped a lot. "We want to take care of him, remind him to bring his coat along when we go East, things like that," said teammate Robert Reid.

At the same time, though, Hakeem sometimes found himself the object of his teammates' ribbing. But he took it all in stride. He was not easily intimidated by his teammates or by his opponents.

The Twin Towers—Olajuwon and Sampson—played well together. In his first season with the NBA, Hakeem averaged 20.6 points and 11.9 rebounds. Sampson averaged 22.1 points and 10.4 rebounds.

It was quite a feat for two teammates, one of them a rookie, to average more than 20 points and 10 rebounds each. The Twin Towers became the first pair to accomplish this since Wilt Chamberlain and Elgin Baylor of the 1970 Los Angeles Lakers.

Hakeem is congratulated by teammate Ralph Sampson after a victory over the Boston Celtics on June 1, 1986. Together, Hakeem and Sampson were called the Twin Towers.

Bernard King, a player for the New York Knicks, said that facing them "is like shooting a basketball into the forest. You know you've got a good chance of hitting a branch." King was referring to their long arms, which they easily stretched out to interfere with the shots of opposing teams.

Hakeem's first season with the Rockets was good not only for Hakeem but also for the team. With 48 wins and 34 losses, the team finished second in the NBA Midwest Division. (The Midwest and Pacific divisions form the Western Conference.) The Rockets had earned a spot in the NBA playoffs. But the team's hopes of a championship ended quickly. In the first round, Hakeem and the Rockets lost to the Utah Jazz.

Hakeem's individual achievements did not go unnoticed, however. He was runner-up for Rookie of the Year. The award went to another talented new-comer—Michael Jordan. But it was clear that Hakeem had almost effortlessly jumped over another obstacle and was headed for success in the NBA.

After his first NBA season, everyone realized what a great asset Hakeem was to the Rockets. Ray Patterson, the team's general manager, praised Hakeem's skills on the court.

"People just didn't know there would be someone with that combination of strength, size, and quickness at the center position," said Patterson.

During his second season, Hakeem played even better. He led the Rockets to a 51–31 record, securing the Midwest Division title. The Rockets were in the NBA playoffs once again. In the first round, the Rockets easily defeated the Sacramento Kings in three games. In the second round, they beat the Denver Nuggets in six games.

Then the Rockets faced a very tough opponent— the Los Angeles Lakers. The Lakers were the defending NBA champions. And leading the Lakers were basketball greats Kareem Abdul-Jabbar and Magic Johnson. But the Lakers still could do nothing against

Magic Johnson reaches for the ball as Hakeem falls on the court during a game between the Los Angeles Lakers and the Rockets on May 21, 1986.

the unstoppable Twin Towers. The Rockets finished off the Lakers in only five games.

Magic Johnson was impressed by Hakeem. "In terms of raw athletic ability, Hakeem is the best I've ever seen," he said.

With Hakeem's help, the Rockets had made it into the 1986 NBA finals. Now came their greatest challenge yet—Larry Bird and the Boston Celtics. Bird was considered one of the best players ever in the NBA. He had been named Most Valuable Player for the third year in a row. And he had already helped the Celtics win several NBA championships.

Hakeem and the Rockets played well, but Bird and the Celtics simply took the game to a higher level. In six games the Celtics defeated the Rockets to win another championship for Boston.

Of course Hakeem and his teammates were disappointed. But Hakeem had been playing with the Rockets for only two seasons. He was sure that in the years to come, the team would have many more opportunities to win a championship. Hakeem could not know, however, that a long and rocky road lay ahead between the Rockets and an NBA victory.

Chapter 5

Seasons of Disappointment

The years after the 1986 NBA championship were not great for the Houston Rockets. One problem was that Ralph Sampson was often sidelined with injuries. Early in the 1987–1988 season, he was traded to the Golden State Warriors. The team still made it to the playoffs each year between the 1986–1987 season and the 1990–1991 season. But the Rockets always lost in an early round.

Despite these frustrations, Hakeem became the first player to place among the NBA's top ten in scoring, rebounding, blocked shots, and steals for two consecutive seasons. He was also selected for several All-NBA First Teams, NBA All-Defensive First Teams, and Western Conference All-Star teams.

Hakeem also experienced great joy in his personal life. In 1988 he became a father. His daughter's name is Abisola, which means "born in joy for all." Hakeem and Abisola's mother, Lita Spencer, had been college sweethearts.

Although Hakeem and Lita are no longer together, Hakeem sees Abisola as much as possible. He once said, "My life right now is very simple. What's impor- tant to me is God, my daughter, and basketball."

By now it was clear that Hakeem would be stay- ing in Houston for a long time. He decided to have a house of his own built.

"I wanted it to be casual but elegant," he said. So Hakeem's home is a one-story, white stucco house with two bedrooms.

A lover of art, Hakeem owns a collection of mas- terpieces by abstract artists. When designing his home, Hakeem kept the placement of this art in mind. Besides collecting art, Hakeem occasionally enjoys oil painting and horseback riding.

Hakeem stands in front of his dream house.

Hakeem has many other interests besides basketball, including horseback riding.

On the basketball court, Hakeem achieved an amazing feat on March 29, 1990. In a game against the Milwaukee Bucks, he earned a quadruple-double. A quadruple-double means that a player scores two-digit figures in four categories. Hakeem had 18 points, 16 rebounds, 11 blocked shots, and 10 assists.

Triple-doubles (two-digit figures in three categories) have become fairly common in recent years, but quadruple-doubles are very rare. In fact, Hakeem became only the third player in NBA history to record a quadruple-double. Playing for the Chicago Bulls, Nate Thurmond recorded the first quadruple-double back in 1974. And Alvin Robertson, who played for the San Antonio Spurs, had one in 1986.

During the 1990–1991 basketball season, Hakeem suffered a serious injury. It happened on January 3, 1991, when, in a game against the Chicago Bulls, Chicago center Bill Cartwright collided with Hakeem. Cartwright's elbow caught Hakeem in the eye, and Hakeem crumpled to the floor in pain. The blow had fractured the bones surrounding Hakeem's eye.

On January 14, Hakeem had surgery on his eye. Afterward doctors felt confident that Hakeem would be fine. He was confident, too. After all, hadn't he overcome so many obstacles already? However, he had to be patient. He would not be allowed to play basketball until his eye healed completely. Hakeem missed 25 games in a row while he was recovering. When he returned to the court, he wore goggles to protect his eye from further injury.

Although Hakeem continued to play exceptionally well, the Rockets continued to be mediocre. In 1992, for the first time in Hakeem's career, Houston did not make the NBA playoffs.

Hakeem became frustrated with the way he was being treated by the Houston management. He felt that his salary did not reflect his value to the team. Things were so bad that Hakeem even asked to be traded to another team. But at the beginning of the

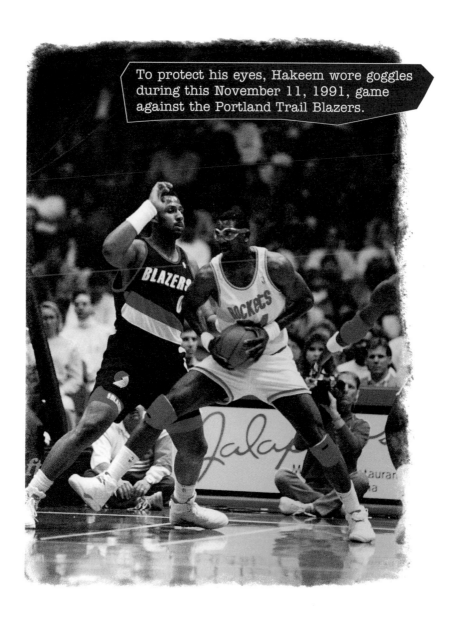

To protect his eyes, Hakeem wore goggles during this November 11, 1991, game against the Portland Trail Blazers.

1992–1993 season, the two sides worked out their differences. The Rockets offered Hakeem a new and better contract, and their star center agreed to stay in Houston. Yet Hakeem's life was about to undergo another change.

Chapter 6

A Renewed Faith

By now basketball had become the center of Hakeem's existence. Although he enjoyed playing the game, it had become somewhat routine. And even though he had money and fame, he was not as happy as he thought he would be.

"I had a life," Hakeem recalled, "but something was missing." Then an event occurred that would have a profound effect on Hakeem. "I found a mosque in Houston." (A mosque is a Muslim temple.) "When I heard the call to prayer, I got goose bumps. And I knew, this is what's been missing."

Although Hakeem had been brought up as a Muslim, religion had not been a big part of his life. Now, however, he realized how important his faith was to him. He vowed to renew it.

Hakeem now prays five times every day. On Fridays he goes to the mosque to pray. And every year, after basketball season has ended, Hakeem travels to Mecca, the Muslim holy city in Saudi Arabia. Hakeem goes there to thank Allah for his good fortune. (*Allah* means "god" in Arabic.) Whenever he travels with the

Hakeem's renewed faith has given him happiness and peace.

Rockets, Hakeem takes along a prayer rug and a compass. He uses the compass to point him in the direction of Mecca as he prays.

With his renewed faith Hakeem is happier and has found inner peace. In the past he sometimes displayed a bad temper on the basketball court. He also complained about Houston's management and about his salary. Now, however, he does not become so angry or upset when things don't go his way.

"My religion is a faith of peace," says Hakeem. "Studying about how we are supposed to live has helped me understand how I should live."

Even basketball is no longer just routine. "Now, it's an act of worship," says Hakeem. "My talent comes from Allah. It's my duty to develop it."

Another duty that Hakeem takes seriously is being a good role model. "It is a responsibility to set an example," says Hakeem. "You don't do it for others, but for yourself."

In 1993 Hakeem made an important personal decision. He decided to become a United States citizen. "I felt I owed America a great debt," he wrote in his 1996 autobiography, *Living the Dream: My Life and Basketball.* He had lived in the United States for many years. He also knew that he had been given many valuable opportunities and achieved incredible success in this country.

Hakeem has a special place in his heart for young fans. During a business trip to Southeast Asia in September 1994, he signed autographs at a shopping mall in Kuala Lumpur.

"People in America treated me like one of their own," he wrote. "To show my gratitude and that I was honored to be treated so graciously, I wanted to become a citizen." Hakeem was sworn in as a U.S. citizen on April 2, 1993.

Like other sports stars in the United States, Hakeem is frequently asked to endorse various products. Basketball players are often asked to lend their names to promote expensive sneakers. Hakeem, however, is selective about the products he represents. When Spalding asked the Houston star to endorse a new line of its sneakers, he gave the offer a great deal of thought.

Hakeem was worried about lending his name to advertise sneakers that many people could not afford. "How can a poor working mother with three boys buy sneakers that cost $120?" he said. "She can't. So kids steal these shoes from stores and from other kids. Sometimes they kill for them." So Hakeem worked with the sneaker company to develop affordable shoes. His "Dream" sneakers sell for only $35.

Hakeem also feels a responsibility to help others. He created the Dream Foundation to help young people in Houston. Each year the foundation provides college scholarships for five high school seniors. The students are chosen based on their good grades, community service, and personal drive.

Hakeem feels that doing good not only benefits others but also benefits him. "The real value of your

Hakeem feels a responsibility to help others, especially children.

talent," Hakeem wrote in his autobiography, "is how you use it to do good and to encourage others. . . . With that I feel rich, not in material things but for what I have inside myself. The richness of the soul."

Back on the basketball court, Hakeem and the Rockets were playing better than ever. They were still waiting to win an NBA title, though. But to Hakeem, a championship victory now seemed somehow less necessary. With his renewed faith came a renewed joy in simply playing the game. He realized that he would be happy with or without an NBA crown.

"I won't compete with other players over who has more money or more commercials or more championship rings," he promised. "If they have more, so be it. I am happy and satisfied and content and grateful for what I do have."

Interestingly enough, Hakeem would soon have an opportunity to achieve his long-sought goals.

Chapter 7

The Thrill of Victory

The 1992–1993 season was a fantastic one for Hakeem. He was named NBA Defensive Player of the Year for the first time in his career. Also, under their new coach, Rudy Tomjanovich, the players really began to click as a team. With a 55–27 record, they won the Midwest Division. This qualified them for the NBA playoffs. Although the Rockets lost in the Western Conference semifinals, they had a terrific season.

The Rockets soared into the 1993–1994 season, winning their first 15 games. They continued to play well all year. With a record of 58–24, Houston won the Midwest Division for the second season in a row.

Hakeem had a great season as well. His scoring average was 27.3, the best of his career. He ranked fourth in the league for rebounds and second for blocked shots. And for the first time, Hakeem was named the NBA's Most Valuable Player. He also received the NBA Defensive Player of the Year award for the second consecutive year.

In the playoffs the Rockets' first opponents were the Portland Trail Blazers. Houston beat Portland in

Hakeem blocks a shot by New York Knicks' center Patrick Ewing during game three of the 1994 NBA finals. The Rockets won 93–89.

four games. The second round against Charles Barkley and the Phoenix Suns was not so easy. The series went all the way to seven games, but the Rockets were victorious. Hakeem scored an unbelievable 37 points in the final game.

When the Rockets met the Utah Jazz in the conference finals, it was no contest. The Rockets triumphed in five games. For the first time since 1986, Houston was headed for the NBA finals.

In the finals Hakeem and the Rockets faced their toughest opponents—Patrick Ewing and the New York Knicks. The stage was set for a matchup between Hakeem and Ewing. Neither of these big men had ever won a championship in his professional career. Both were hungry for victory. Professionally, this was the last obstacle for Hakeem to overcome.

Houston was the setting for the first two games of the series. There the Rockets and the Knicks each won one game. Then the series moved to New York for three games. The Rockets took the first game, but the Knicks won the next two.

When the series returned to Houston, the Knicks led three games to two. They needed to win only one more game to end the Rockets' dreams of a championship for yet another season. Game six was breath-stoppingly close. With less than one minute remaining, the Rockets were leading by only two points. The score was 86–84. In the last few seconds, the Rockets missed a shot. The Knicks now had an opportunity to tie or win the game.

Knicks' guard John Starks had the ball. He was behind the three-point line. If he made the shot, the Knicks would score three points to win not only the game but also the championship. But just as Starks went for the shot, Hakeem jumped up and tapped the ball. As the buzzer signaled the end of the game, Starks' shot missed the basket. Hakeem's block had saved the game for Houston!

Now the series was tied at three games apiece. Game seven, to be played in Houston, would decide which team would win the 1994 NBA championship. The Knicks played well, but Hakeem and his teammates soared. When the game was over, the Rockets had won their first NBA title with a score of 90–84.

The fans in Houston went wild! They rushed down from the stands onto the floor. They were running and jumping, shouting and smiling. "My celebration was to watch everybody being ecstatic, rejoicing, jumping on tables and hugging each other, showing emotion in their own way," Hakeem later recalled.

Victory was very sweet for Hakeem. It was the first time any professional team in Houston (basketball, baseball, or football) had won a major title. "I'm so happy to bring a championship to Houston," he said afterward.

Hakeem was awarded the trophy for Most Valuable Player in the NBA finals. He then became the first player in NBA history to be named regular-season MVP, Defensive Player of the Year, and finals MVP in the same season.

The 1994–1995 season should have been a good one for the defending NBA champions. But it was not one of Houston's best. Trades and injuries made it a trying year for the team.

After the regular season, the Rockets were seeded only sixth in the Western Conference. However, Hakeem had an amazing run during the playoffs. He averaged 33 points, 10.3 rebounds, and 2.85 blocks. Hakeem and his teammates rallied to win their second NBA title in a row.

The Houston Rockets became the lowest-seeded team ever to win a championship. The Rockets also became one of only five NBA teams to win back-to-back titles. The other teams were the Boston Celtics, Chicago Bulls, Detroit Pistons, and the Los Angeles Lakers.

In the 1995–1996 season, the Rockets hoped to win a third straight NBA championship. However, injuries plagued many of the team's top players. Knee problems had forced Hakeem to sit out ten games at the end of the regular season.

Before his injuries, though, Hakeem had gone down in the record books. He passed Kareem Abdul-Jabbar to earn the NBA career record for number of blocked shots. Hakeem also became only the ninth player in NBA history to collect more than 20,000 points and 10,000 rebounds in his career.

The Rockets' 48–34 record qualified the team for the playoffs. Their first opponents were the legendary Magic Johnson and the Los Angeles Lakers. The Rockets defeated the Lakers and moved on to face the Seattle Supersonics. The Sonics, however, proved to be too much for the Rockets. Seattle won the series, dashing the Rockets' hopes for a third NBA title.

After the 1995–1996 basketball season ended, Hakeem traveled to Atlanta, Georgia. He was thrilled to participate in the 1996 Summer Olympics. Because he had become an American citizen, he was playing basketball for the United States. He felt proud to represent his adopted country. "It's a chance to demonstrate not just our talent, but our character, to the world," Hakeem said.

Hakeem's teammates included Shaquille O'Neal, Charles Barkley, David Robinson, Grant Hill, Karl Malone, and Scottie Pippen. With such great basketball stars playing together, the U.S. team was once again nicknamed the "Dream Team."

The United States was heavily favored to win, and they did not disappoint their fans. Hakeem and the Dream Team took home gold medals for the United States.

As gold-medal winners, each team member received a $15,000 bonus. All 12 members of the Dream

On their way to Olympic gold in 1996, Hakeem and the rest of the Dream Team beat China.

Team donated their bonuses to charities. Hakeem gave his bonus to the Islamic Society of Greater Houston.

In 1996 Hakeem's personal life changed dramatically when he decided to get married. Hakeem followed the Islamic tradition of prearranged marriage. That means that his bride was chosen for him. Hakeem did not even meet his future wife until after the marriage had been arranged. She was the daughter of a man who worshiped at the same Houston mosque as Hakeem did.

"There is no dating process, no boyfriends and girlfriends in Islam," explained Hakeem. "Families meet, talk, get to know one another. Then, the marriage is arranged." Hakeem married Dalia Asafi a few weeks after the 1996 Olympics.

Shortly after the 1996–1997 season began, Hakeem had a scare. In the middle of a game against the Washington Bullets, his heart began to beat wildly. Hakeem left the game and was taken to the hospital. There the doctors found that he had atrial fibrillation. With this condition, the heart beats as much as five times faster than normal. As a result Hakeem now takes medicine to keep his heart from beating too fast. Doctors say that his condition will not affect his basketball career or his life.

So it looks as if Hakeem will continue to play professional basketball for at least a few more years. He has worked hard for a long time and finally achieved his dream of winning a championship—not once but twice. For some time he has also been recognized as one of the best players ever in the NBA.

But these achievements are not what is most important to Hakeem. In his autobiography he wrote, "I want to be remembered as a great person; not the greatest player in the world but a person who was honest and gracious and honorable. . . ."

Perhaps, too, he will be remembered as the young man who began to play basketball at an age most American players think is too old. And perhaps he will also be remembered as a man of quiet determination who gracefully made the huge adjustment of mastering a culture very different from his own.

Hakeem Olajuwon's
Career Highlights

1980 Moved to the United States and enrolled at the University of Houston on a basketball scholarship.

1982 Led Houston Cougars to NCAA Final Four (semifinal round).

1983 Led Houston Cougars to NCAA finals.

Named MVP of the NCAA tournament.

1984 Led Houston Cougars to second consecutive NCAA finals.

Entered the NBA; selected as first draft choice by the Houston Rockets.

1985 Was runner-up for Rookie of the Year award.

1986 Led the Houston Rockets to the NBA finals.

1989 Became the first player to place among the NBA's top ten in scoring, rebounding, blocked shots, and steals for two seasons in a row.

1990 On March 29, became only the third player in NBA history to record a quadruple-double.

1991 Missed 25 games due to eye injury and surgery.

1993 Became a United States citizen on April 2.

Named NBA Defensive Player of the Year.

Was runner-up for regular-season MVP award.

1994 Led the Houston Rockets to their first NBA championship.

Became first player in NBA history to be named regular-season MVP, Defensive Player of the Year, and finals MVP in the same season.

1995 Led the Houston Rockets to their second consecutive NBA championship.

Named NBA finals MVP for the second consecutive year.

Passed Kareem Abdul-Jabbar's record to become the NBA's all-time shot blocker.

1996 As part of the U.S. Dream Team, won a gold medal in basketball at the Olympics.

Further Reading

Gutman, Bill. *Hakeem Olajuwon: Superstar Center.* Brookfield, CT: Millbrook, 1995.

Harvey, Miles. *Hakeem Olajuwon: The Dream.* Chicago: Children's Press, 1994.

Knapp, Ron. *Sports Great Hakeem Olajuwon.* Hillside, NJ: Enslow, 1992.

Kramer, Sydelle. *Hoop Stars.* New York: Grosset & Dunlap, 1995.

Mullin, Chris, and Brian Coleman. *The Young Basketball Player.* New York: Dorling Kindersley, 1995.

Olajuwon, Hakeem, and Peter Knobler. *Living the Dream: My Life and Basketball.* Boston: Little, Brown, 1996.

Rekela, George R. *Hakeem Olajuwon: Tower of Power.* Minneapolis: Lerner, 1993.

Vancil, Mark. *NBA Basketball Basics.* New York: Sterling, 1995.

Withers, Tom. *Basketball.* Austin, TX: Raintree Steck-Vaughn, 1994.

Index